# SERGIO ARAGONÉS ON PARADE

Edited by
## ALBERT B. FELDSTEIN
with
## JERRY DE FUCCIO

WARNER BOOKS

A Warner Communications Company

WARNER BOOKS EDITION

**Copyright** © 1961, 1962, 1963, 1964, 1965, 1966, 1967, 1968, 1969, 1970, 1971, 1972, 1973, 1974, 1975, 1976, 1977, and 1978 by Sergio Aragonés and E. C. Publications, Inc.

Warner Books, Inc.,
75 Rockefeller Plaza,
New York, N.Y. 10019
A Warner Communications Company

Title "MAD" used with permission of its owner, E. C. Publications, Inc.

*Designed by Thomas Nozkowski*

Printed in the United States of America

**First Warner printing:** September 1982
10  9  8  7  6  5  4  3  2  1

**Library of Congress Cataloging in Publication Data**

Aragonés, Sergio.
    Mad's Sergio Aragonés on parade.

    Originally published as: Sergio Aragonés on parade.
    1. United States—Social life and customs—Caricatures and cartoons.   2. Spanish wit and humor, Pictorial.
I. Feldstein, Albert B.    II. De Fuccio, Jerry.
III. Mad.    IV. Title.
NC1639.A63A4  1982       741.5'946       82-10883
ISBN 0-446-37369-9 (U.S.A.)
ISBN 0-446-37487-3 (Canada)

# The Creations Of Sergio

## *by Jerome A. DeFuccio*
(With a tip of the sombrero to Robert W. Service
for writing "The Cremation Of Sam McGee")

*There are strange things done 'neath the tropic sun
By the men who draw cartoons.
They make grand designs with their squiggly lines
Through the sun-baked afternoons.
In the dusty haze of those blazing days,
There are queer things seen, I know:
But the sight to beat in that Latin heat
Was the young lad Sergio.*

Now, young Sergio lived in Mexico
Where the enchiladas bloom,
And the boy-cows gore every matador
'Til there's death in the afternoon.
In that fabled land of the taco stand
Even saintly padres swore
The mustachio grown by Sergio
Sprouted out when he was four.

With his awesome look, he was oft' mistook
For the dashing Cisco Kid;
But a hero he couldn't hope to be,
With those wild cartoons he did.
Soon, his parents knew they must tell him true
To vamoose that lovely land,
And go be the clown in some Gringo town,
Once he'd swum the Rio Grande.

Thus did Sergio flee from Mexico,
But this tale grows still more sad:
To compound disgrace, once he'd left the place,
He was called to work for MAD.
How this came to be isn't hard to see,
No one else but MAD would look
At cartoons so wee they could only be
In the margins of the book.

Now, it's quite a show watching Sergio
Do those tiny things he draws.
How his pen will dart through each work of art,
Done without one moment's pause.
While the paper twirls, he makes whirling swirls
That soon form a wordless jest.
Some are long and tall; some are wide and small,
Each is drawn with Latin zest.

After year on year of his MAD career,
Sergio's now first in rank
Among men of art who fill the part
That most magazines leave blank.
Still, despite the strain, traits of youth remain,
And he often draws a glance
On Manhattan streets as some friend he greets
With a svelte flamenco dance.

*There are strange things drawn in New York's gray dawn
By the men who do cartoons.
They can't sleep a wink, so they dab with ink
In their cold and lonely rooms.
Soon their youth will go. But not Sergio!
He shines brightly as before.
And enjoys the grind, for in each fan's mind
He's a grand conquistador!*

# CONTENTS

# VISITING DAY

As Americans, one of our most admirable traits is the ability we have to laugh at ourselves and make light of serious matters. Even Cape Canaveral couldn't escape the humorous onslaughts directed its way by such comics

# A MAD LOOK AT THE

# U.S. SPACE EFFORT

Sergio Aragones, who recently arrived at MAD from Mexico, made his début
with the hilarious "A MAD Look at the U.S. Space Effort," and is currently

# A MAD LOOK AT M

filling our margins with his delightful "Drawn-Out Dramas," now points
his satirical pen at a usually un-funny U.S. phenomenon, and gives us

# OTORCYCLE COPS

Sergio Aragones, MAD's newest addition, who recently arrived from "South Of 1
Border"—and contemplated making for it when his "MAD LOOK AT MOTORCYCLE COP

# A MAD LOOK

published, now takes his satirical pen in hand and brings us this humorous
raisal of our quaint "Fall Saturday Afternoon Sports Spectacles". Here is:

# AT FOOTBALL

# THE SMALL BUSINESSMAN

# Who Knows What Evils Lurk In
# THE SHADOW

# he Hearts Of Men?
# KNOWS

LOVE
THY
NEIGHBOR

# AT THE CIRCUS

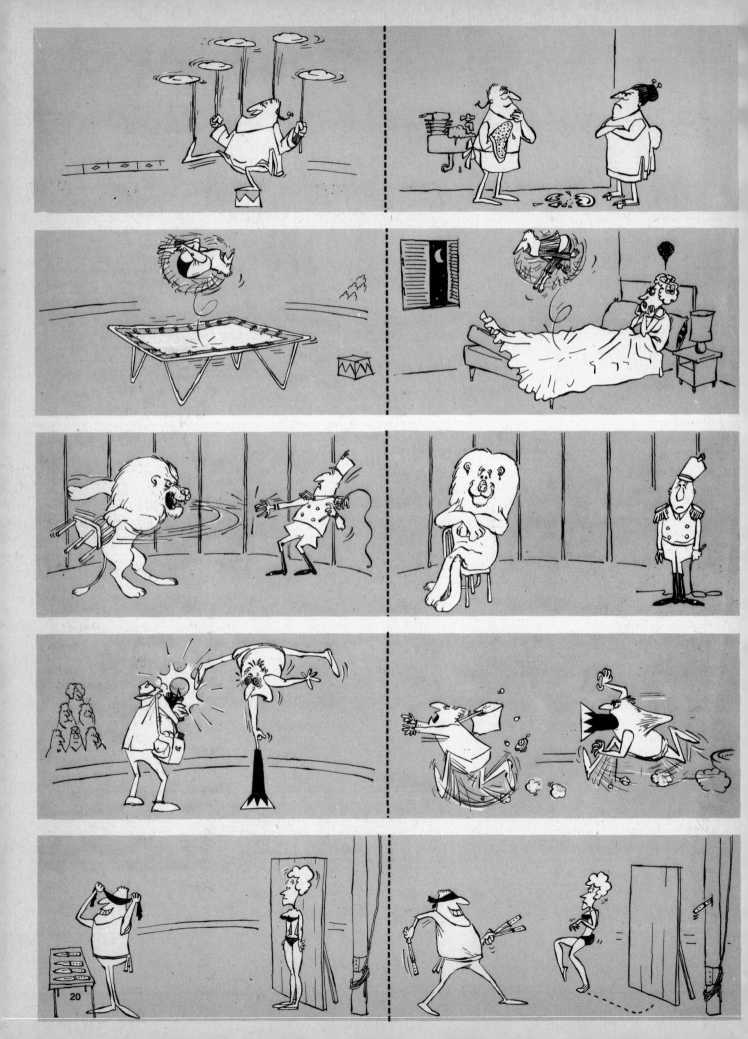

20

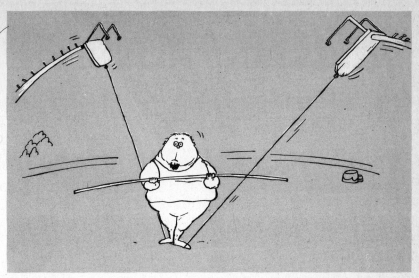

21

# RUSSIAN "RUSSIAN ROULETTE"

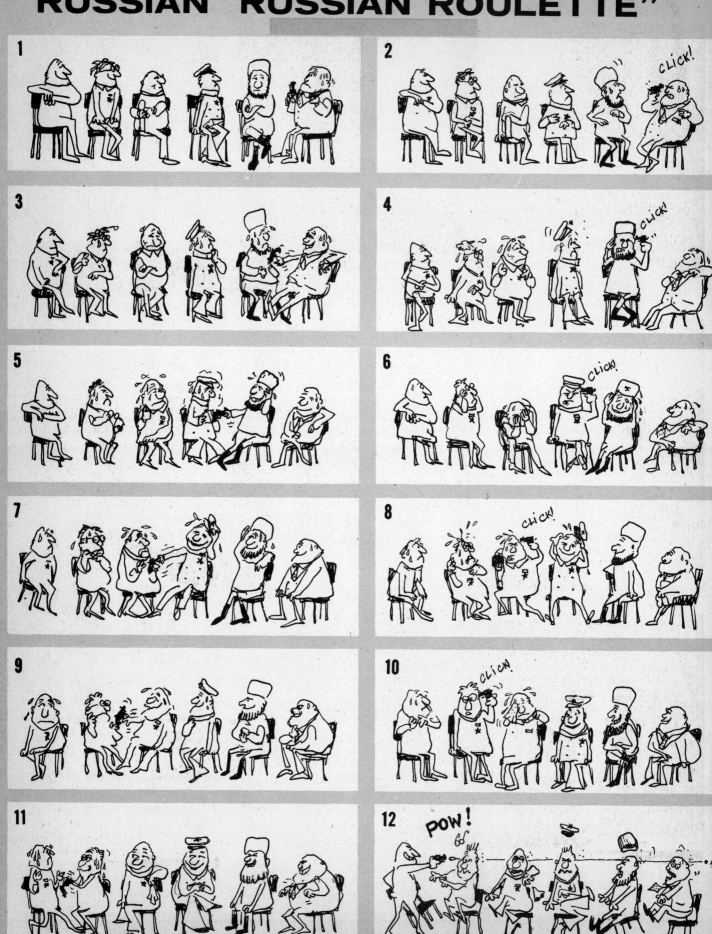

# ALLEY-OOPS!

# A MAD LOOK

# AT FIREMEN

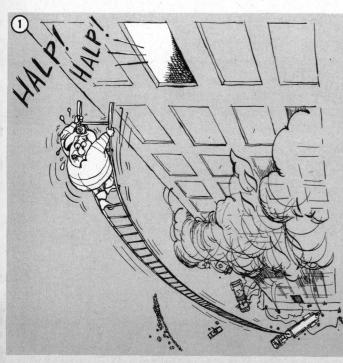

# THE PROBLEM

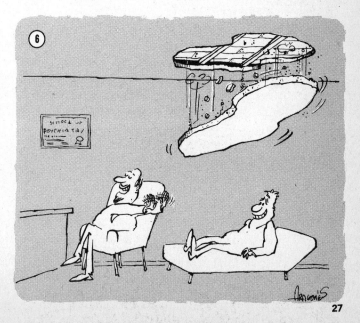

# THE NIGHTMARE

# THE HEIST

MORE

# A MODERN FAIRY TALE

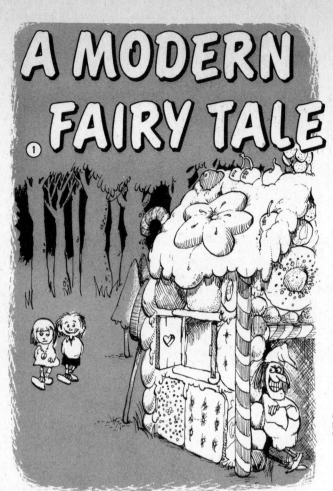

NO PRESERVATIVES ADDED
NO ARTIFICIAL COLORING
100% PURE ORGANIC
NO CYCLAMATES

# A MAD LOOK AT THE

# UMMER OLYMPICS

WRESTLING

# A MAD LOOK AT

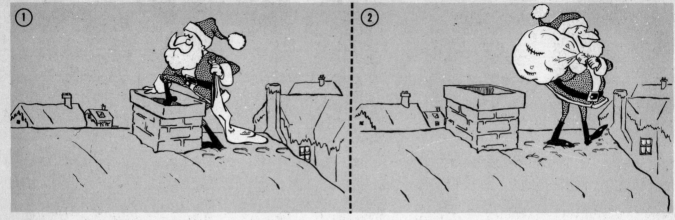

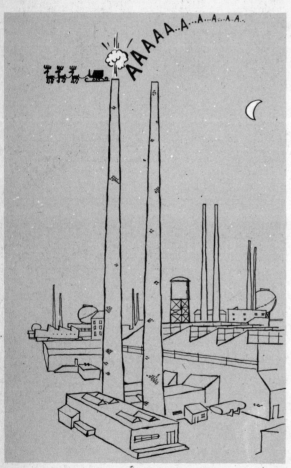

# A MAD LOOK

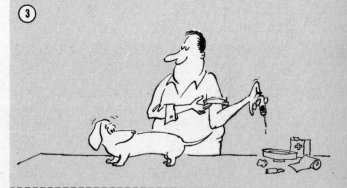

# AT DOGS

# THE GREAT ESCAPE PLOT

# ON THE ROAD

## with Sergio Aragones

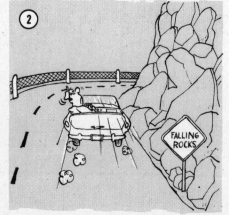

# Who Knows What Evils Lurk In
# THE SHADOW

WET PAINT

# The Hearts Of Men?
# KNOWS

# A MAD LOOK AT AMUSEM

# ENT PARKS

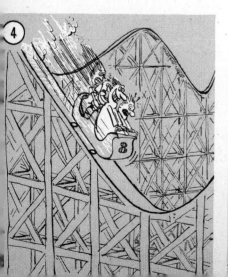

ARAGONÉS 51

# ON THE WAY TO THE POLICE COSTUME BALL

# WHAT IS A

ARTIST : SERGIO ARAG

**B**etween the time you watch your first Lawrence Welk TV Show on your Daddy's knee, and the time you finally settle down in a Retirement Village to live on your Social Security, you are guaranteed to run across a creature called a "Square". Squares come in four basic styles: Dull, Very Dull, Boring, and Ed Sullivan.

**S**quares are found almost everywhere: In the ping-pong room at the YMCA, perusing the menu at a Howard Johnson's, being paged at a Trailways Bus Station, taking a sight-seeing tour and staring up at the tall buildings . . . in Fargo, North Dakota, and tapping their feet and shouting, "One more time!" to the music of Guy Lombardo.

**I**t's easy to spot a Square—simply by the way he dresses. Who else would wear mis-matched argyle socks, thermal underwear, a chartreuse bolero bowling shirt, a plaid woolen hat with earlaps, J. C. Penney slacks with pleats, a graduation ring with a squirter attachment, and a clip-on wide tie that lights up in the dark and says: "Philadelphia is a fun city!"—all to his own wedding?!

**A** Square is Simplicity waiting in line at the "Don McNeill Breakfast Club," Banality chug-a-lugging Ovaltine at a Rexall counter, Tedium thumbing through a Spiegel's Mail Order Catalogue, and the Height of Idiocy marching in a Shriners' Parade, playing "Zip-A-Dee-Doo-Dah" on a kazoo.

**A** Square's idea of romance is a kiss—on the fifth date . . . from his wife. A Square's idea of high-brow entertainment is a videotape replay of "The Gale Storm Show." A Square's idea of a culinary treat is to send out for some Chicken Delight. A Square's idea of nostalgia is seeing Snooky Lanson stepping into the "Lucky Strike Spotlight." And a Square's idea of the height of adventure is tearing down the goalposts at the end of a football game.

# SQUARE?

WRITER: ARNIE KOGEN

**A** Square is never a Jazz Musician, or a Peace Corps Worker, or an Abstract Artist, or a Las Vegas Croupier, or a member of the Jet Set. He is always an Accountant, or a Ticket-Tearer at a Roller Derby Tournament, or a Zeppelin Repairman, or a Blotter Salesman, or a President of a Wayne Newton Fan Club.

**A** Square is a composite of many people: He has the rugged authority of Don Knotts, the sardonic wit of Bud Collyer, the magnetic personality of Lyndon Johnson, the poise of Huntz Hall, the quiet good taste of Allen & Rossi, the sex-appeal of Chet Huntley and the flashiness of Dean Rusk.

**A** Square is unique in many ways: He's the one wearing a "Harold Stassen for President" button. He's the one who starts a Conga line and "dips" when he dances. He's the one who goes into a fancy French Restaurant and asks the waiter, "What's the hot cereal?" He's the one who throws his friend a Bachelor Party at a McDonald's Hamburger Stand. And he's the one who still reads "National Geographic" for the "hot parts"!

**C** ontemporary terminology often confuses a Square. He thinks "White Backlash" is a Revlon cosmetic, a "Stag Film" is a movie about Bambi, a "Pink Lady" is a Communist sympathizer's wife, "The Mamas and The Papas" is a Planned Parenthood Group, and a "Good Night Kiss" is a small Hershey you eat before retiring.

**M** ight as well face it, Squares are here to stay. They may try to disguise themselves and act like "Hippies," but some of their Squareness will always show through. They can discard their galoshes, hide their Bennett Cerf Humor Anthologies, stop watching "Supermarket Sweep" and discontinue their Hammond Organ lessons, but there will still be one thing that gives them away . . . the tell-tale phrase that always separates the Square from the rest of the world . . . the War-Cry of the Square Make-Out Man:

**"HUBBA HUBBA!"**

# A MAD PEEK BEHIND

ARTIST: SERGIO ARAGON

discover what new and inventive ways we the people are being shafted. Won't you join us for

# THE SCENES At A Fancy Restaurant

WRITER: LARRY SIEGEL

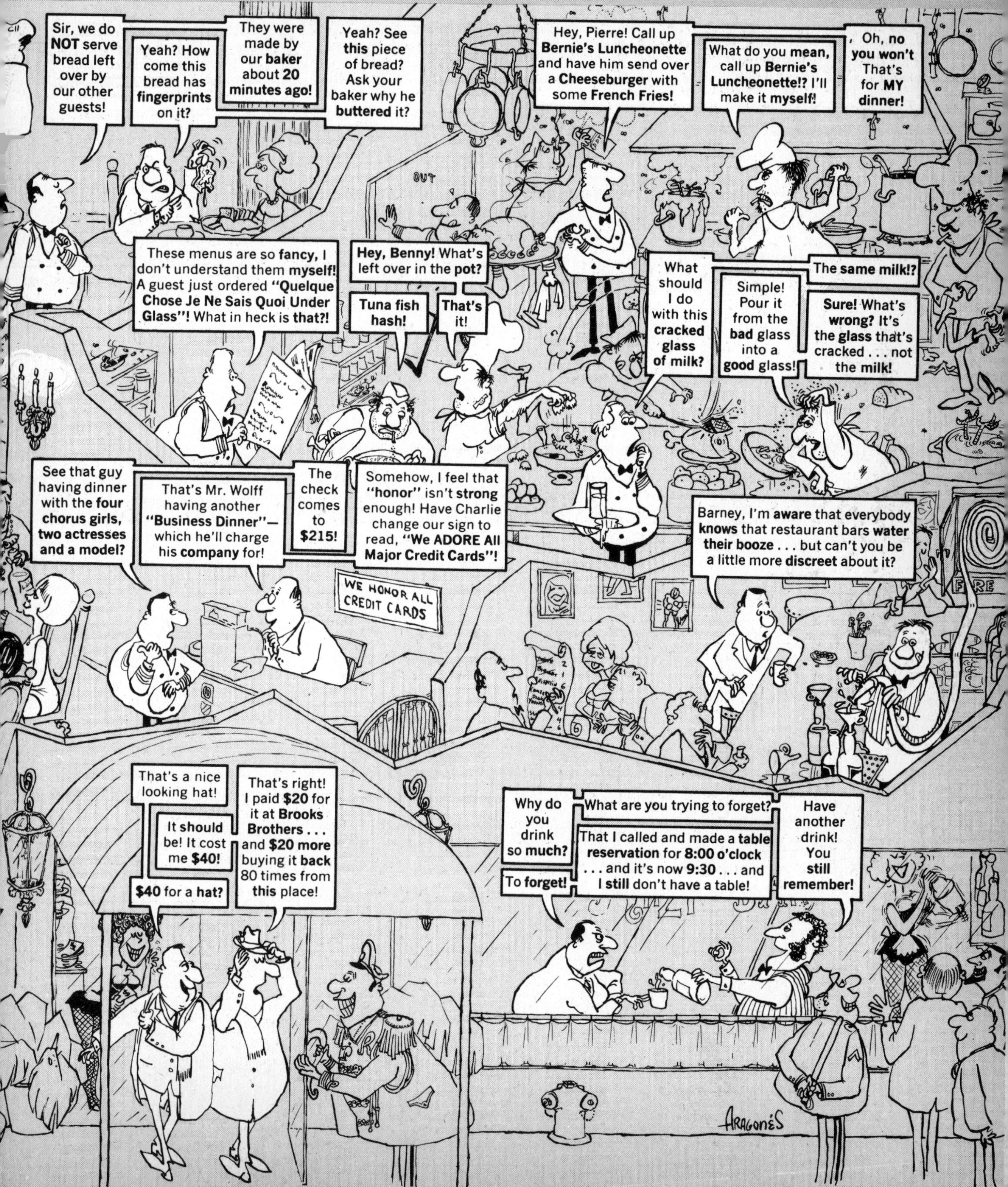

# WHAT IS A B

ARTIST: SERGIO ARAGON

**B**etween the time you're slapped on the back in Maternity, and the time you're slipped on the slab in the Mortuary, you're bound to run into that remarkable creature known as a "Born Winner". It's simply unavoidable. Born Winners require a never-ending supply of poor slobs like you and me to use as stepping stones on their way to the top.

**S**ome people have the mistaken notion that Born Winners are just plain lucky. Nothing could be further from the truth. The word luck implies that it can be either good or bad. For a Born Winner, this is impossible. His luck always turns out to be good no matter how bad it may appear at any given moment. Not only do all his clouds have silver linings, but also the clouds themselves are pure gold.

**A** Born Winner is easy to spot. He's the guy who's drafted the morning the war ends. He's the guy who marries for love and then discovers his bride concealed the fact that she's a millionairess to avoid fortune hunters. He's the guy who's turned away from a fancy restaurant for not wearing a tie the very same night that thirty-six diners succumb to food poisoning.

**C**oincidence plays a large role in a Born Winner's life . . . and guess in whose favor? When a Born Winner goes in to ask for a raise, you can bet it's the morning after the Boss made it with the gorgeous new secretary. When a Born Winner has to exchange his tickets for a Hit Show to another night, you can bet he's avoided the night both stars are replaced with understudies. When a Born Winner decides to try another route to work for the first time in ten years, you can bet it's the day rioters burn fifteen cars along the old route.

**I**n one strange way, a Born Winner needs to be pitied. For the rest of us, one of life's thrills is its uncertainty. This thrill is denied the Born Winner. He always knows how things will turn out. If he kicks a dog in front of the ASPCA Shelter, he knows he'll wind up being rewarded for dislodging a bone in its throat. If he loses

# RN WINNER?

ER: AL JAFFEE

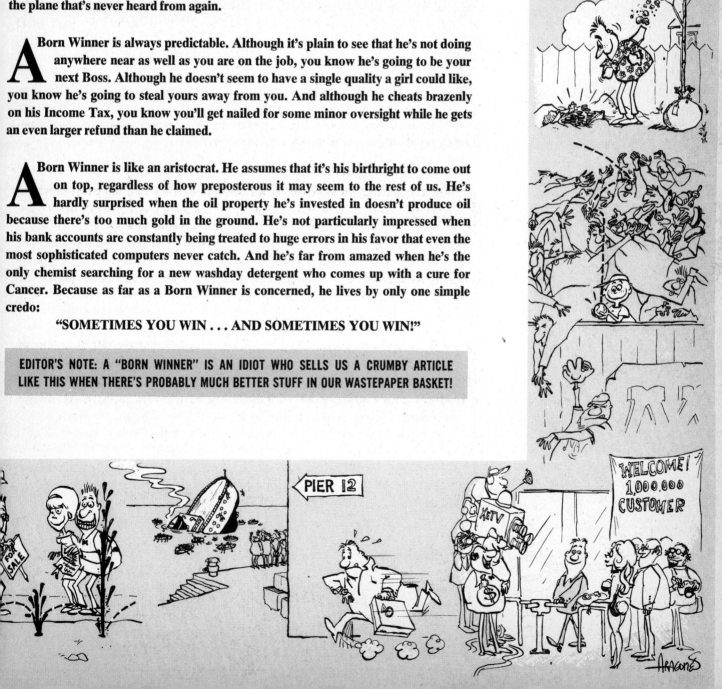

a sweetheart to a rival, he knows she'll turn out to need $11,000.00 worth of medical and dental care. And if his wife buys what looks like a worthless piece of junk at an auction, he knows it's going to turn out to be a priceless Cellini original.

**S**ometimes, it's incredible how victory is snatched from the jaws of defeat by Born Winners. If a Born Winner is stuck with huge alimony payments, his ex-wife promptly marries the milkman. If a Born Winner's car turns out to be a lemon, it's immediately stolen and the insurance money pays for a new one. If a traffic cop is about to give a Born Winner a ticket, a burglar alarm suddenly goes off somewhere down the street. And if a Born Winner is bumped off a plane by a VIP, that's the plane that's never heard from again.

**A** Born Winner is always predictable. Although it's plain to see that he's not doing anywhere near as well as you are on the job, you know he's going to be your next Boss. Although he doesn't seem to have a single quality a girl could like, you know he's going to steal yours away from you. And although he cheats brazenly on his Income Tax, you know you'll get nailed for some minor oversight while he gets an even larger refund than he claimed.

**A** Born Winner is like an aristocrat. He assumes that it's his birthright to come out on top, regardless of how preposterous it may seem to the rest of us. He's hardly surprised when the oil property he's invested in doesn't produce oil because there's too much gold in the ground. He's not particularly impressed when his bank accounts are constantly being treated to huge errors in his favor that even the most sophisticated computers never catch. And he's far from amazed when he's the only chemist searching for a new washday detergent who comes up with a cure for Cancer. Because as far as a Born Winner is concerned, he lives by only one simple credo:

### "SOMETIMES YOU WIN . . . AND SOMETIMES YOU WIN!"

EDITOR'S NOTE: A "BORN WINNER" IS AN IDIOT WHO SELLS US A CRUMBY ARTICLE LIKE THIS WHEN THERE'S PROBABLY MUCH BETTER STUFF IN OUR WASTEPAPER BASKET!

# WHAT IS A E

**B**ETWEEN THE TIME you first toddle across a Nursery, and the time you last stumble into a Nursing Home, you are certain to step on a low form of Human Life called a "Born Loser." It's unavoidable. Born Losers are always underfoot, waiting to get hit on the head by every misfortune the rest of the world drops.

**S**OME PEOPLE WASTE years trying to help Born Losers change their luck. But it's useless, because Born Losers are born to lose, and they merely transform those who attempt to do something about it into Losers themselves. Born Losers drive their Psychiatrists into psychoses, their Employment Counselors into unemployment, and their Driving Instructors into ambulances . . . head-on!

**I**T'S EASY TO SPOT a Born Loser. He's the one who rushes into traffic to rescue a confused puppy, and gets a ticket for jaywalking. He's the one whose car horn gets stuck just as he's beginning to make out in a drive-in movie. He's the 999,999th fan to buy a ticket at the ball park on the day the one-millionth wins a Buick . . . and the 10,001st to get in line the day 10,000 World Series tickets go on sale.

**S**TRANGE AS IT SEEMS, the world needs Born Losers. Somebody has to be the Republican Congressional candidate in Lyndon Johnson's home district. Somebody has to pitch for the Chicago Cubs. And somebody has to go to Frank Sinatra's hotel room and tell him the other guests are complaining about the noise.

**B**ORN LOSERS TRADE drought-stricken farms for houses in towns that are immediately demolished by flash-floods. Born Losers never hear prowlers ransacking their living rooms because they're making too much racket upstairs installing burglar alarms. Born Losers starve themselves into malnutrition in order to afford the premiums on Health Insurance Policies that cover every illness but malnutrition.

# ORN LOSER?

WRITER: TOM KOCH

**S**OMETIMES IT ALMOST SEEMS that Born Losers go out of their way to avoid good fortune. They're lucky enough to get Bob Dylan's autograph . . . and then unlucky enough to drop it in a mud-puddle. They're lucky enough to work for a company with a generous retirement program . . . and unlucky enough to have the company go bankrupt the week before they turn 65. They're lucky enough to win a Summer Vacation in Scandinavia . . . and unlucky enough to be stranded there for the Winter by an airline strike.

**I**N A WAY, BORN LOSERS are to be envied. They seem to be capable of accomplishing things by accident that few of us could do on purpose. Who but a Born Loser could get his rain check at a called-off double-header too soggy to be redeemed? Who but a Born Loser could find a rare 1894 dime in his change, and then put it into a pay phone to call home with the good news? Who but a Born Loser could hit a 270-yard golf shot out of the rough, over a creek, through some trees, onto the green and into the cup . . . of the wrong hole?

**T**HE NICEST THING ABOUT a Born Loser is that he's so predictable. Even before the door prize drawing is held, you know he bought the winning ticket and lost it. Even before he finishes building his new home, you know the state will condemn the land it's on for a throughway. And even before he's sidestepped that last tackler on his 98-yard touchdown run, you know the whole play will be nullified by the referee.

**B**UT THROUGH IT ALL, the Born Loser remains a creature of indomitable spirit. He may be the only guy ever to have thieves steal his car and leave the hub caps. He may be the only guy to amass a great fortune and then invest it in Trans-Cuba Airlines. And he may be the world's only phone subscriber who's forced to share a four-party line with a bookie joint, a doctors' answering service and an all-night drug store. Still, nothing shakes a Born Loser's conviction in the creed he lives by:

### OH, WELL . . . YOU CAN'T WIN 'EM ALL!

# I REMEMBER

## THE WONDROUS WOODSTOC

# REMEMBER

## MUSIC FAIR

ARTIST: SERGIO ARAGONES
WRITER: FRANK JACOBS

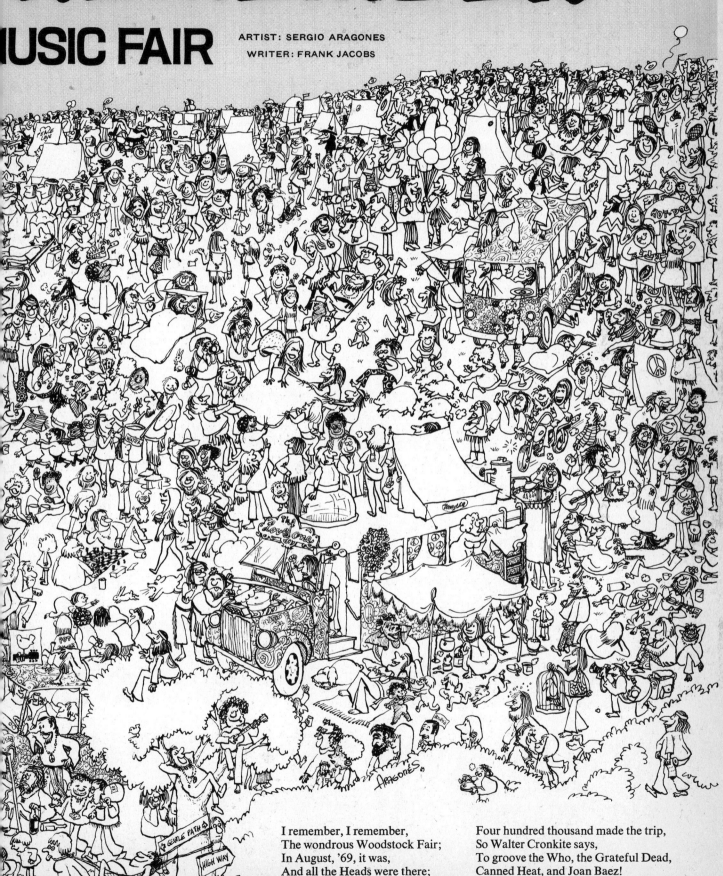

I remember, I remember,
The wondrous Woodstock Fair;
In August, '69, it was,
And all the Heads were there;

Four hundred thousand made the trip,
So Walter Cronkite says,
To groove the Who, the Grateful Dead,
Canned Heat, and Joan Baez!

I remember, I remember,
The traffic unforseen
That clogged the lanes for countless miles
On Highway 17;
And even while I write this verse
I fear there is no doubt
That many drivers still are there
Attempting to get out!

I remember, I remember,
That bleary, bombed-out mass
That wandered 'round the countryside
Freaked out on hash and grass;
Not all of them, I wish to say,
Possessed a glassy stare;
A few, in fact, could still recall
The reason they were there!

I remember, I remember,
That groovy, swinging scene,
That field of wheat that soon became
An open-air latrine;
And how it warmed our happy hearts
And filled us with good cheer
To know the farmer wouldn't need
To buy manure next year!

I remember, I remember,
That cataclysmic flood
Of rain that tumbled from the sky
And turned the Fair to mud;
And how the crowd threw off its clothes
And mingled in the bare,
Until the place looked something like
The final scene of "Hair!"

I remember, I remember,
The way my nights were spent;
The pleasure when I bedded down
Inside my little tent;
And how I found, on waking up,
That all men were my brothers;
That I'd been joined throughout the night
By forty-seven others!

I remember, I remember,
The wondrous Woodstock Fair;
But wait—I haven't told you of
The rock that I heard there;
I'd really like to fill you in,
But much to my dismay,
The closest that I got to it
Was seven miles away!

**Here we go with our answer to the National Safety Council's predictions of how many people will be involved in what type major catastrophes. Mainly—**

# THE MAD SAFETY COUNCIL'S PREDICTIONS
## For The Upcoming Labor Day Weekend
### (How many people will be involved in what-type minor catastrophes)

ARTIST: SERGIO ARAGONES      WRITER: STAN HART

| PREDICTION | ◀ 1,700,000 | ◀ 1,800,000 | ◀ 1,900,000 | ◀ 2,000,000 | ◀ 2,100,000 |
|---|---|---|---|---|---|
| Men who will be mistaken for dead but who will actually be watching a N. Y. Mets double-header on TV. | | | | | |
| Girls who will feel miserable and lonely because there are **no fellows** at their resort hotel. | | | | | |
| Girls who will feel miserable and lonely even though there are **plenty fellows** at their resort hotel. | | | | | |
| Kids whose lips will be shredded when they get stuck to frozen Fudgicles. | | | | | |
| Cars that will be stopped by unmarked police cars for reckless driving. | | | | | |
| Unmarked police cars that will be stopped by **other** unmarked police cars for reckless driving. | | | | | |
| Kids who will suffer chlorine blur diving into swimming pools to retrieve their locker keys. | | | | | |
| Parents who will **worry** when they don't see their child getting off the Camp Train. | | | | | |
| Parents who will **cheer** when they don't see their child getting off the Camp Train. | | | | | |
| men who will suffer heat prostration hile wearing mink jackets at fancy els when temperature is in the 90's. | | | | | |
| People who will **vow** to get together with their Summer acquaintances over the Winter. | | | | | |
| People who will **actually** get together with their Summer acquaintances over the Winter. | | | | | |

Here we go with our answer to the National Safety Council's predictions of
how many people will be involved in what type major catastrophes. Mainly—

# THE MAD SAFETY COUNCIL'S PREDICTIONS
## For The Upcoming Christmas Weekend

### (How many people will be involved in what-type minor Catastrophes)

ARTIST : SERGIO ARAGONES          WRITER: STAN HART

| | 1,700,000 | 1,800,000 | 1,900,000 | 2,000,000 | 2,10 |
|---|---|---|---|---|---|
| Fathers who will have fits when they discover **they** must assemble toys they thought came completely assembled. | | | | | |
| Parents who will be heartbroken when their kid ignores that expensive toy and plays all day with the carton it came in. | | | | | |
| People who will go insane trying to find that one defective bulb that caused all the other lights on the tree to go out. | | | | | |
| College kids who will suffer the agonies of boredom fifteen minutes after they arrive home for the holidays. | | | | | |
| Department store Santa Clauses who will catch colds or worse from being kissed by drippy-nosed little kids. | | | | | |
| Kids who will be glad Santa got a cold or worse because he finked them with clothes or books or other useful gifts. | | | | | |
| Husbands who will be punched in the mouth for giving their wives a Lady's Electric Razor for Christmas. | | | | | |
| Secretaries who will be trapped into listening to Accountants tell jokes at Office Parties. | | | | | |
| Kids who will be rushed to doctors after playing "Dr. Jekyll and Mr. Hyde" with their new Chemistry sets. | | | | | |
| Kids who will get head injuries when they discover their Flexible Flyers aren't really very flexible. | | | | | |
| Three year olds who will be bitten by their new puppies. | | | | | |
| New puppies who will be bitten by three year olds. | | | | | |

# Here we go with our answer to the National Safety Council's predictions of how many people will be involved in what type major catastrophes. Mainly—

# THE MAD SAFETY COUNCIL'S PREDICTIONS
## For The Upcoming New Year's Weekend
### (How many people will be involved in what-type minor Catastrophes)

ARTIST: SERGIO ARAGONES     WRITER: STAN HART

| PREDICTION | 1,700,000 | 1,800,000 | 1,900,000 | 2,000,000 | 2,100,000 |
|---|---|---|---|---|---|
| Teenage party-givers who will want to **die** because their parents insist on "joining in the fun." | | | | | |
| Girls who will be shocked to discover that the wild party planned by their boyfriend is actually at **their house.** | | | | | |
| Boys who will be frustrated to learn that the phrase, "Aw, c'mon, it's New Year's Eve!" doesn't get them any further than any other night. | | | | | |
| Old people who will be moved when Guy Lombardo plays "Auld Lang Syne" on TV | | | | | |
| Young people who will be moved when Guy Lombardo plays "Auld Lang Syne," on TV. | | | | | |
| Men who will go crazy trying to figure out a Night Club bill for a party of 24 people. | | | | | |
| Women who will suddenly faint when they hear an off-color joke at a New Year's Eve party. | | | | | |
| men who will become hysterical when they hear the same off-color joke from woman who made believe she fainted. | | | | | |
| Husbands at parties who will put a lampshade on their head while the plug is still in the socket. | | | | | |
| umiliated wives at parties who will arrested for electrocuting husbands who put lampshades on their head. | | | | | |
| oys who will be lonely because they "had the nerve" to ask a girl to a party at the last minute. | | | | | |
| Girls who will be lonely because a boy "had the nerve" to ask them to a party at the last minute. | | | | | |

# WHAT IS AN

**B**etween the time you are first wheeled out in your stroller, and the time you are last wheeled out on a stretcher, you are bound to roll over a large, dull object known as an Introvert. Such near fatal collisions are unavoidable because Introverts always travel down the road of life headed in the wrong direction . . . with their lights turned off. And they never, ever warn you of their approach by blowing their horns.

**I**ntroverts are individuals who spend a lot of time alone, thinking about themselves. Unfortunately, that subject is so limited that they have plenty of idle hours left over to come out and get in other people's way. This most often happens in libraries, where they occupy your favorite seat memorizing chess books in case they should ever be asked to play . . . Or in men's rooms, where they block your view of the mirror while they search for ingrown nostril hairs . . . Or in phone booths, where they make you wait while they try to think of a tactful way to ask "Information" for information.

**N**ot that an Introvert would ever get in your way on purpose. It's just that he seldom notices what's happening around him because he's concentrating so hard on how it makes him feel. He only remembers being at the World Series because that's where a peanut vendor humiliated him for not having the exact change. He only remembers the 1972 election because that's when he didn't vote for fear of doing something stupid at the polling place. And he only remembers wintering in Florida because that's where he heard somebody laugh at the way he looked in swim trunks.

**I**t's strange how Introverts always think other people are noticing them. In actuality, they come across with the same kind of impact that makes Franklin Pierce the one president you always forget about, and the Buffalo Bills the one N.F.L. team you always leave off the list, and George McGovern's fellow senator from South Dakota the one you never heard of . . . even if you live in South Dakota. Truth to tell, if Introverts didn't think about themselves so much, they'd never be thought of at all.

**S**till, it's easy to spot an Introvert in a crowd . . . if you can imagine any conceivable reason for wanting to. He's the one working a crossword puzzle by flashlight at the drive-in movie. He's the one hesitating to turn in a perfect exam paper because he's ashamed of his penmanship. He's the one arriving at the auto salesroom with his check for the full sticker price already made out. He's the one ordering "the works" at Chicken Take-out to celebrate his birthday. And he's the one in Group Therapy whose main problem is a fear of speaking up in Group Therapy.

ARTIST: SERGIO ARAGONES

# INTROVERT?

**B**ut deep down inside, Introverts are much the same as everybody else. They have their driving ambitions . . . to read all fifty volumes of the Harvard Classics before they die. They have their smouldering desires . . . to own the world's biggest collection of Liechtenstein air mail stamps. They have their dreams of glory . . . to win national acclaim for being able to recite all of the state capitals in four minutes flat. They even have their fantasies of sin . . . to flog Zsa Zsa Gabor until she tearfully agrees to shut up and become an Introvert.

**N**o doubt about it. An Introvert is more than just another highly forgettable face masking emotions that run the gamut from hardly any to none at all. An Introvert is also Sincerity drowning in a moist handshake, Flaming Passion swathed in a grey wool muffler, Steel Nerves risking all at solitaire, Daredevil Courage revving up a '63 Rambler, Firm Resolve proclaimed in an apologetic mumble, Attentiveness floating on a cloud of pre-occupation, and Thoughtful Silence . . . lots and lots of Thoughtful Silence.

**A**bove all, the Introvert possesses the gift of Dedicated Perseverance. Who else assembles a ten-thousand piece jig-saw puzzle to get a reproduction of "Anne Hathaway's Cottage" suitable for framing? Who else spends every Christmas exposing himself to the flu so he'll have an honest excuse for staying at home on New Year's Eve? Who else gladly drives from Toledo to Cleveland by way of Omaha rather than beg for a road map at a gas station? And who else wastes his whole lunch hour riding home on the bus just so he can use his own bathroom?

**Q**uite obviously, the world needs Introverts. Somebody has to write those 800-page biographies of medieval French kings. Somebody has to be night watchman for the Navy's mothball fleet. Somebody has to think up the anecdotes that President Nixon tells to display his sense of humor. Somebody has to perpetuate the art of engraving the Lord's Prayer on the head of a pin. And, most important, somebody has to be there pretending to listen while all the Extroverts on earth shoot off their big mouths.

**S**ome people tend to feel sorry for Introverts. This is a total waste of sympathy, when you stop to think about it. After all, nobody ever calls upon an Introvert to coach the neighborhood Little League team, or head up a charity fund raising drive, or ruin his Sunday filling out a golf foursome. He is permitted to go his own way doing what he pleases. And the only thing society ever asks of the Introvert is that he keep uttering his familiar cry that brings joy to all:

**"I WAS JUST LEAVING."**

WRITER: TOM KOCH

# GARBAGEMEN

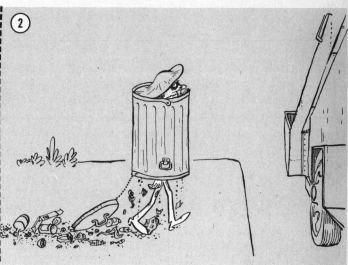

# Who Knows What Evils Lurk In
# THE SHADOW

# KNOWS

# TALES

# THE SKY-JACKER

# SERGIO ARAGONES TAKES A MAD LOOK AT... PROTEST

# DEMONSTRATIONS

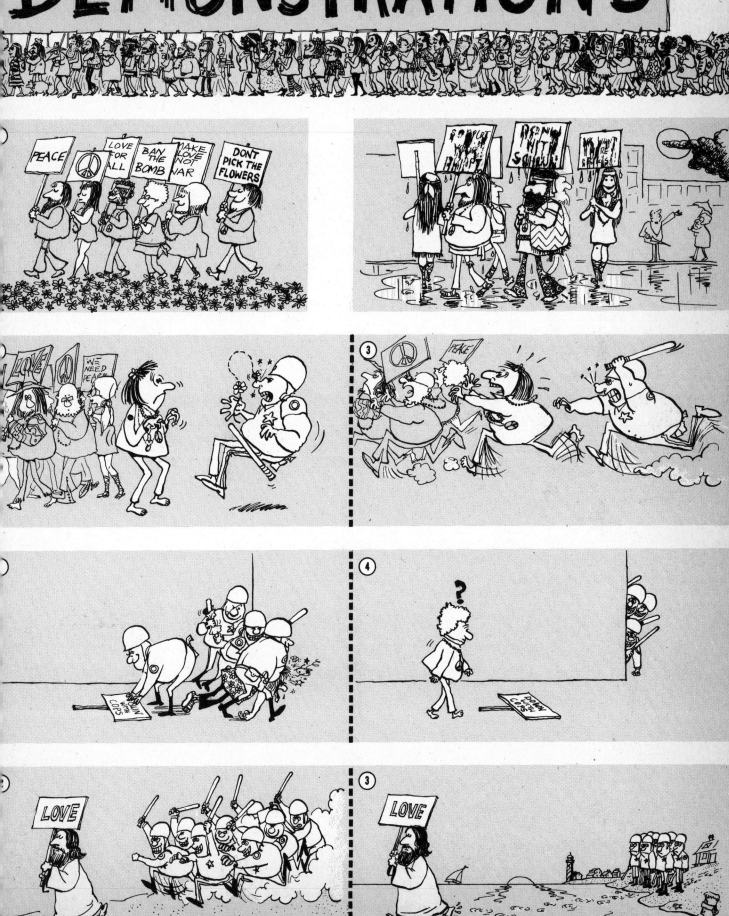

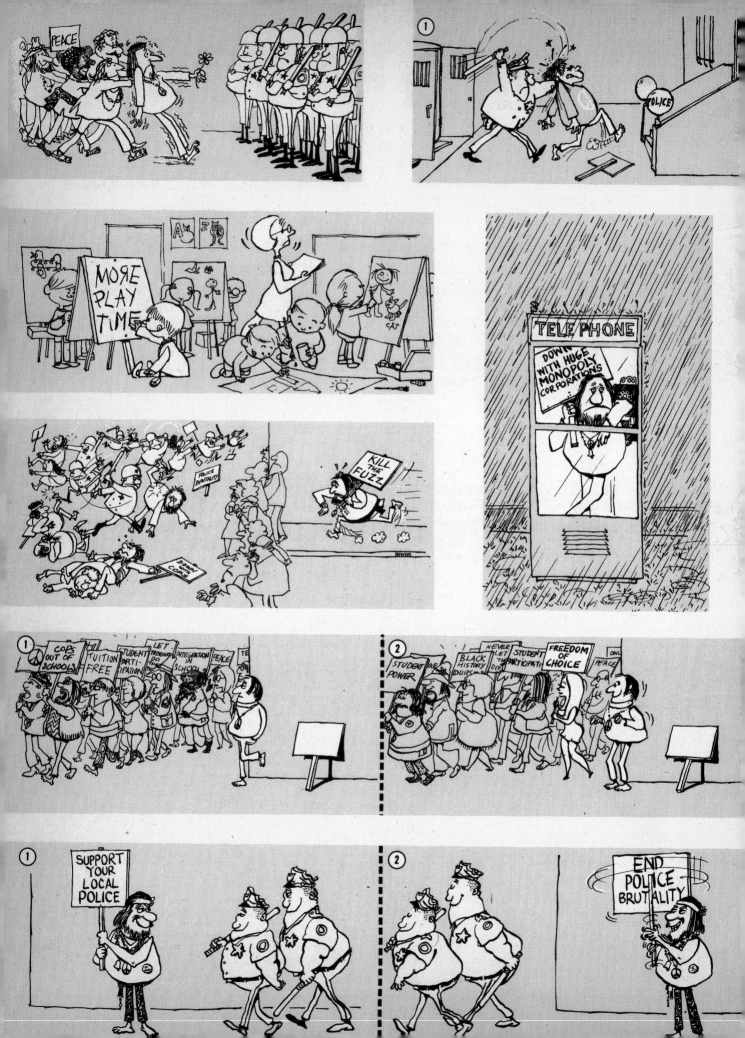

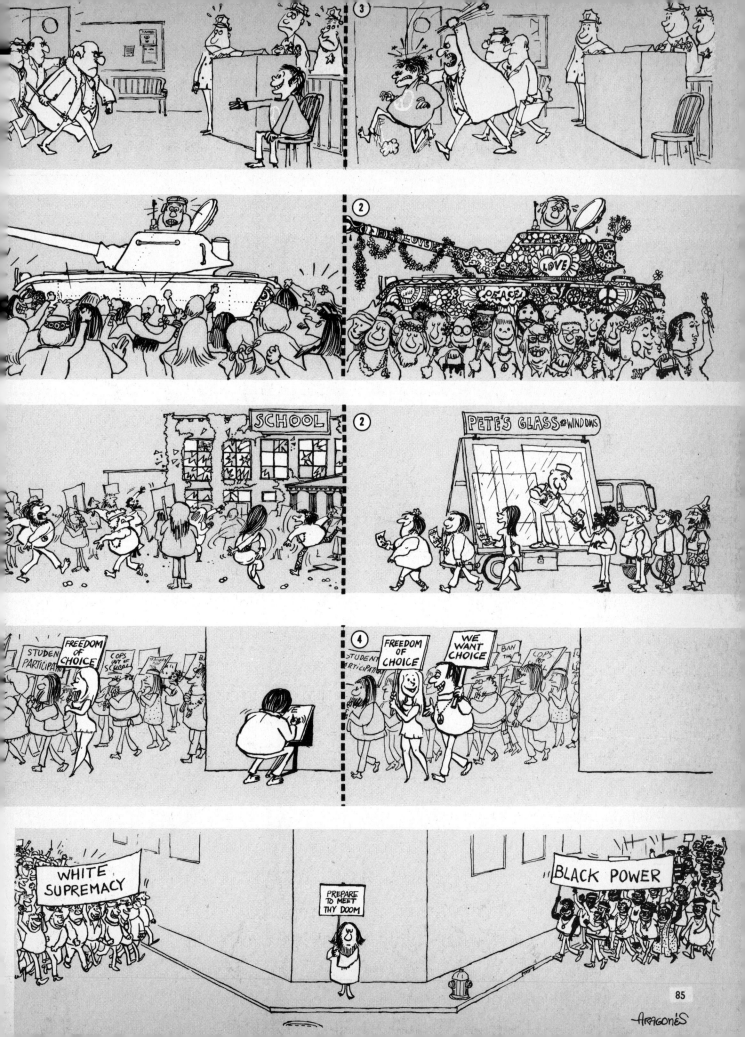

# A MAD LOOK AT WINTER

# PORTS

# A MAD LOOK AT

# AT KARATE

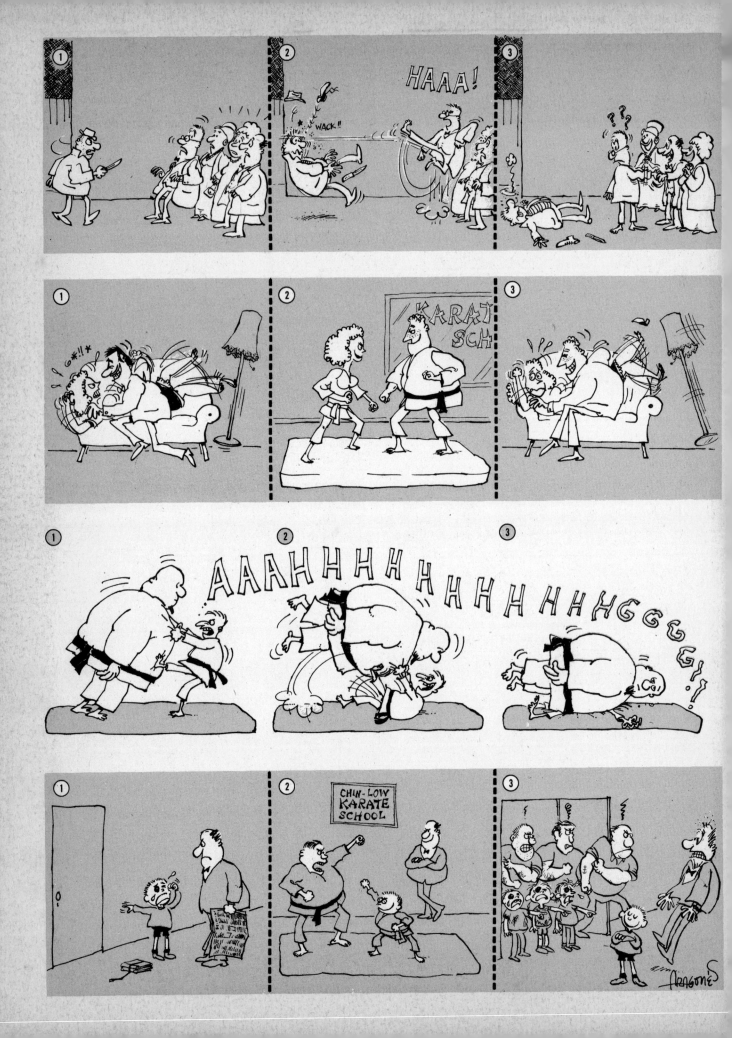

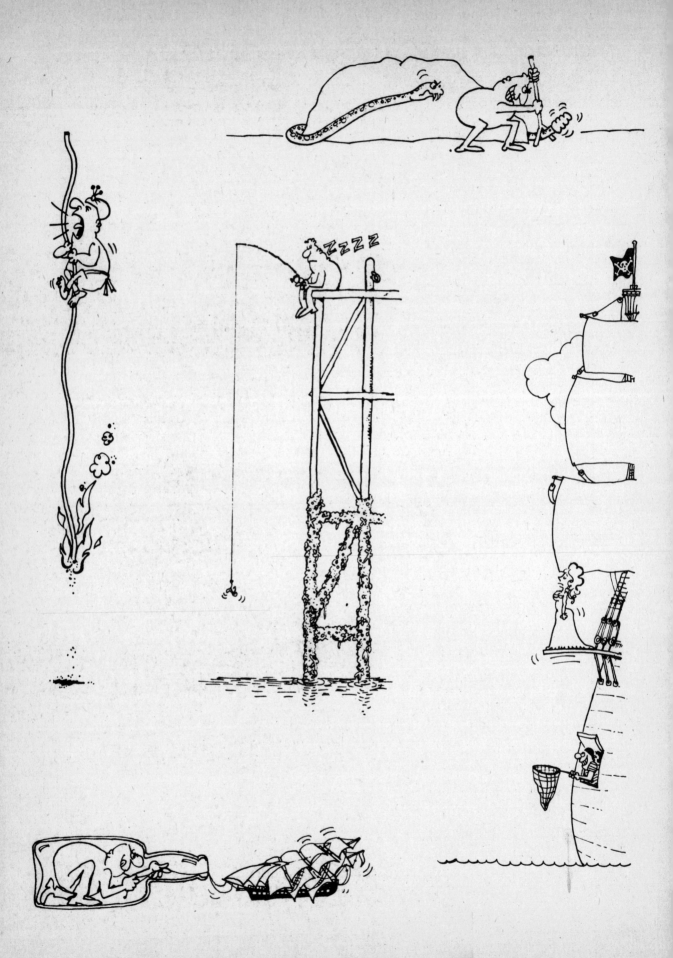

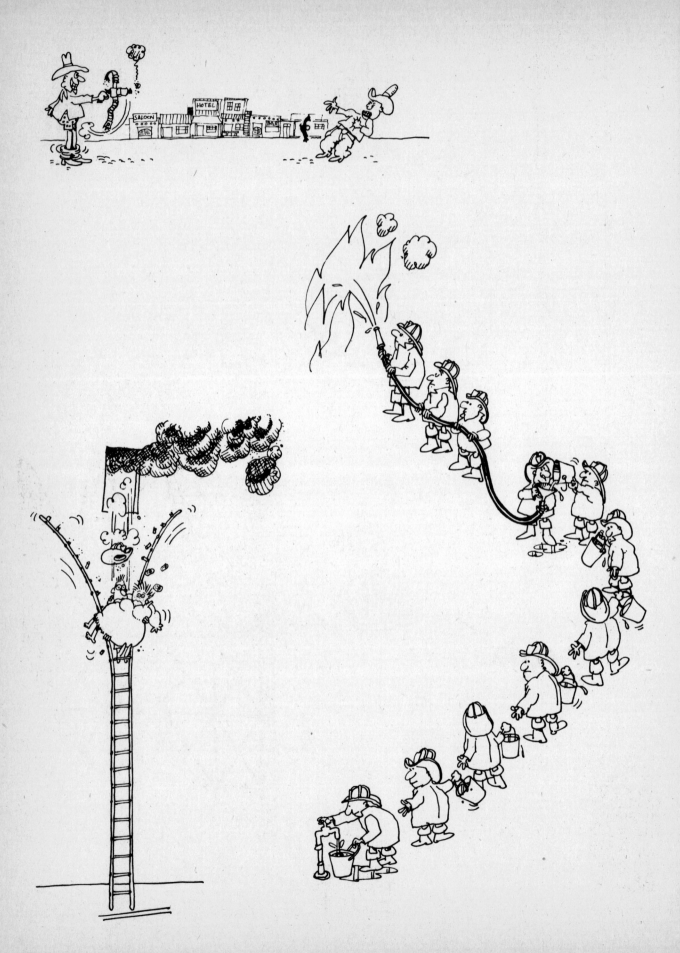

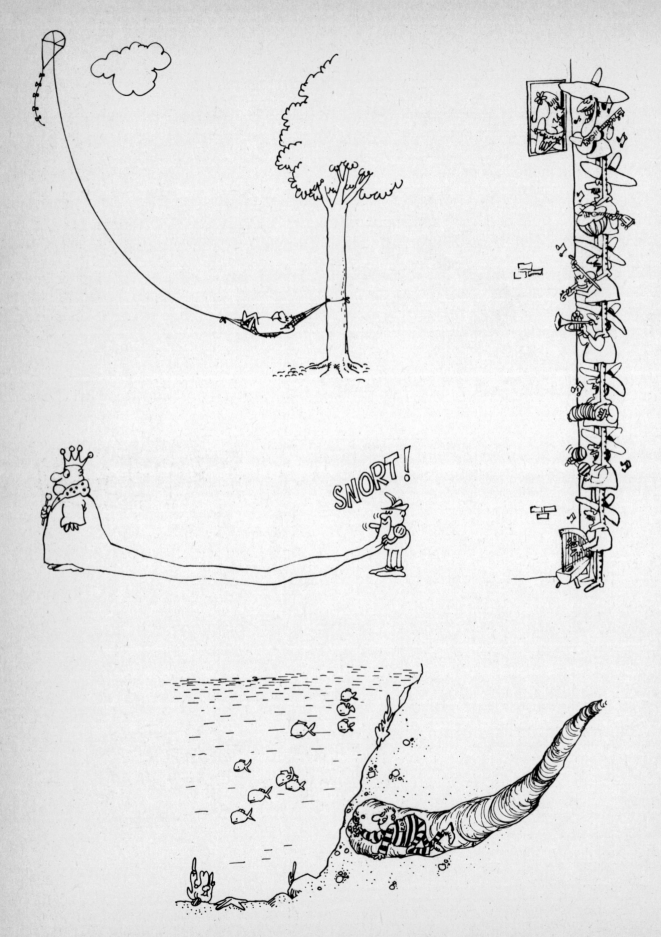

SNORT!

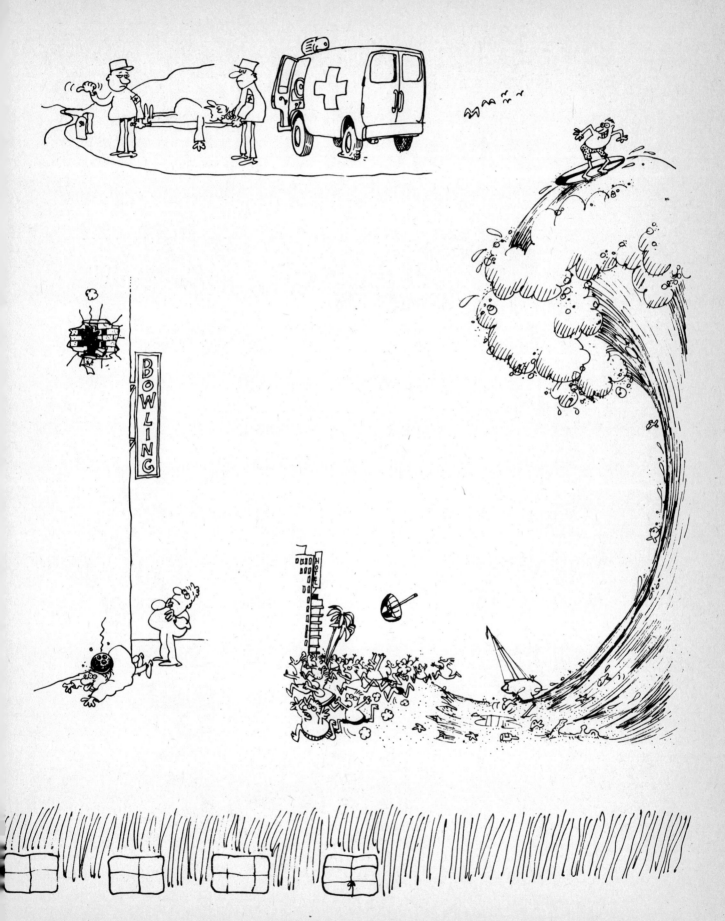

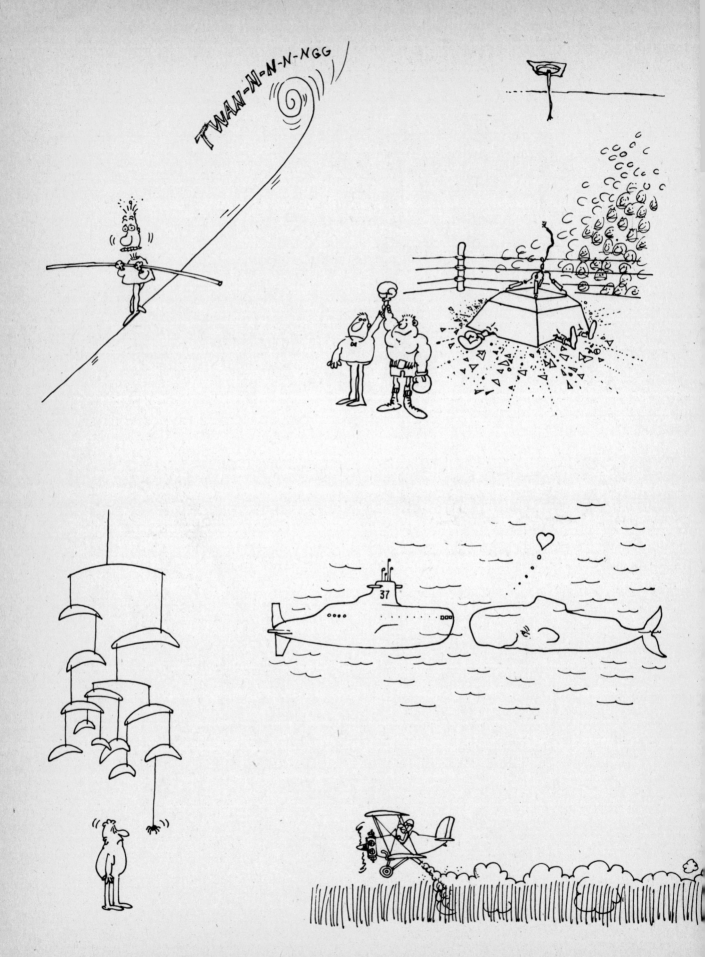

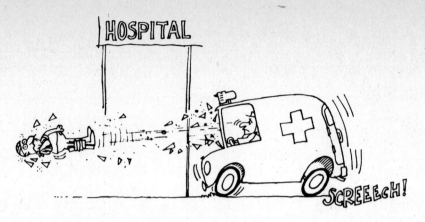

DANGER

# A MAD LOOK AT... HUNT

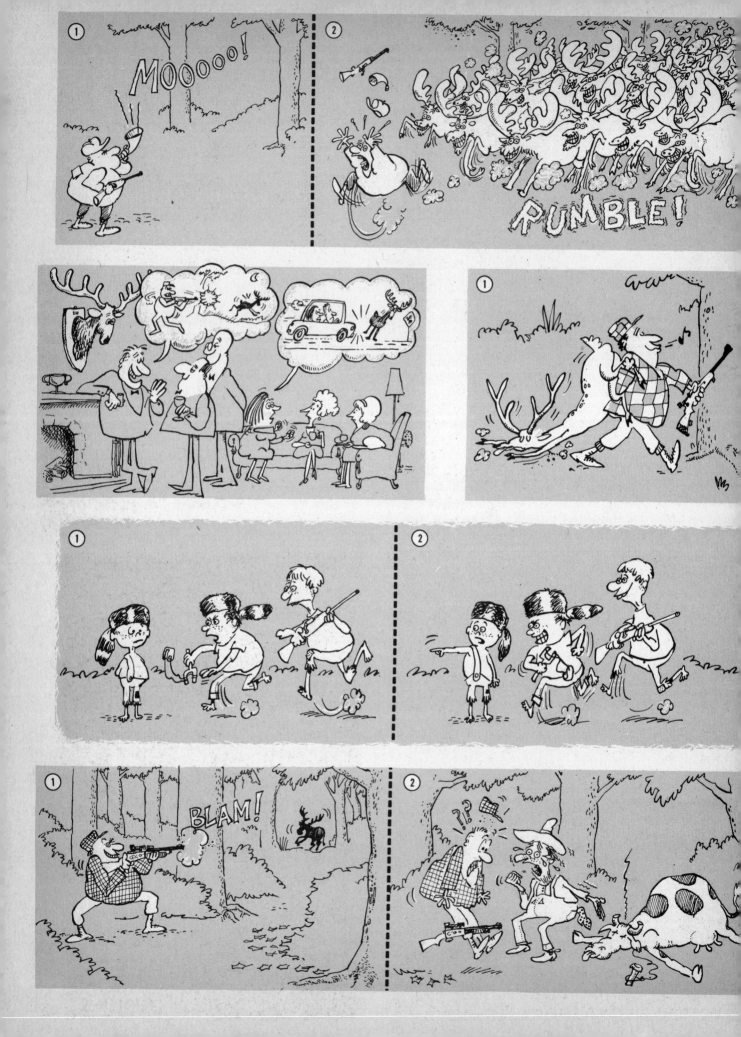

# The Hearts Of Men?
# KNOWS

# MUSICIANS

# MORE POWERFUL THAN A LOCOMOTIVE...

# A MIND-BLOWING INCIDENT

# A MAD LOOK

# AT BIRDS

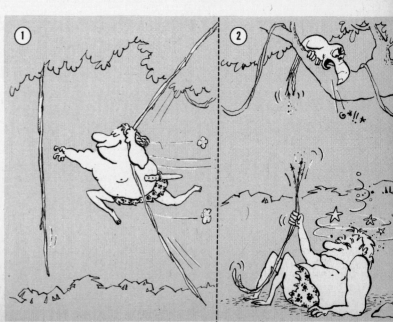

# A MAD LOOK

# AT BICYCLING

# EDDINGS

# MODEL-BUI

# LDING

# THE HISTORIC LANDMARK

# FUTURE SHOCK

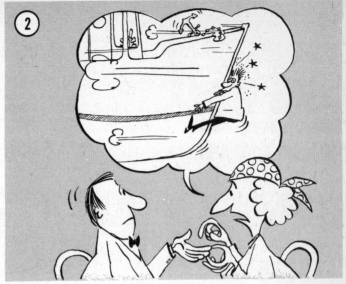

# A COLLECTION OF SELECTED REJECTIONS

Dear Sergio,

Enclosed are the cartoons I didn't use in the article. Mainly because I really have to leave room in the magazine so the <u>other</u> guys can eat.

So don't consider these as "rejections".

Rather consider the ones I used as "selections".

MAD-ly yours,

Al Feldstein

Al Feldstein

Editor

# SOME COVER IDEAS...

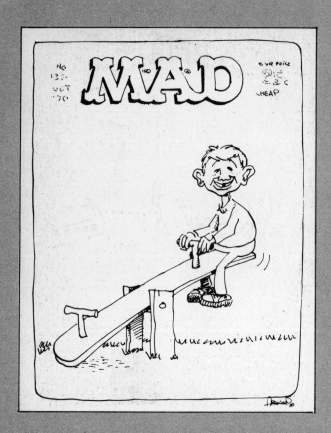

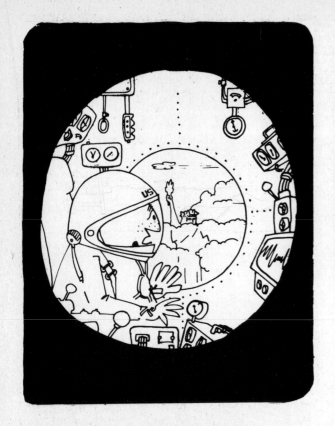

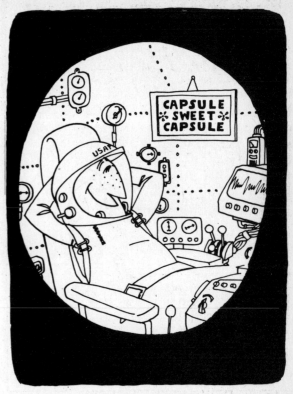

# ...THE LITTLE MATCH GIRL...

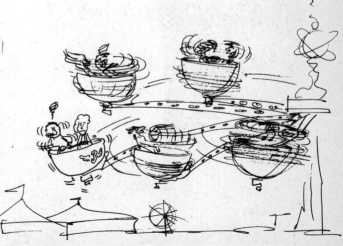

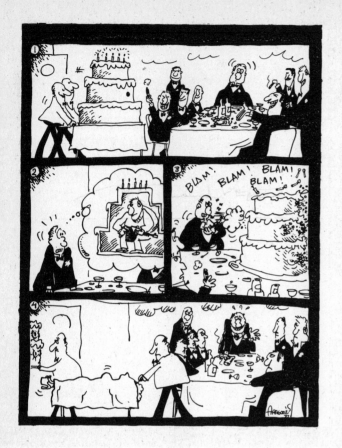

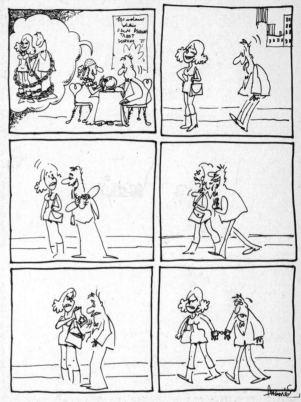

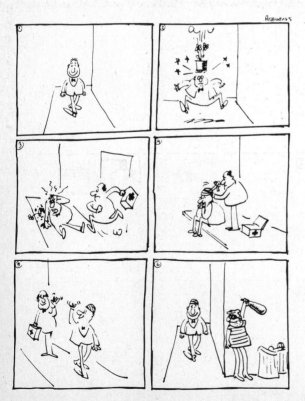

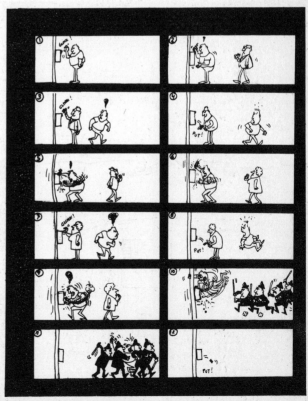

# ...AND SHADOWS

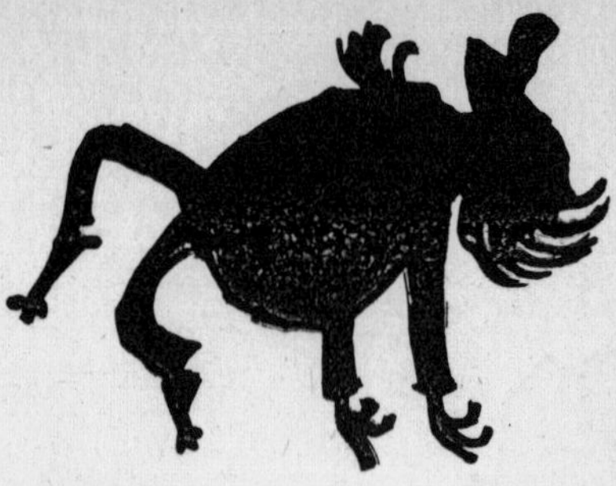

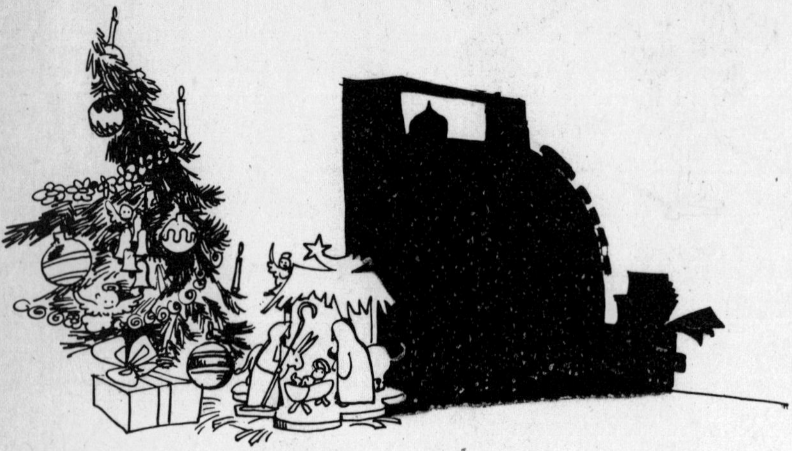

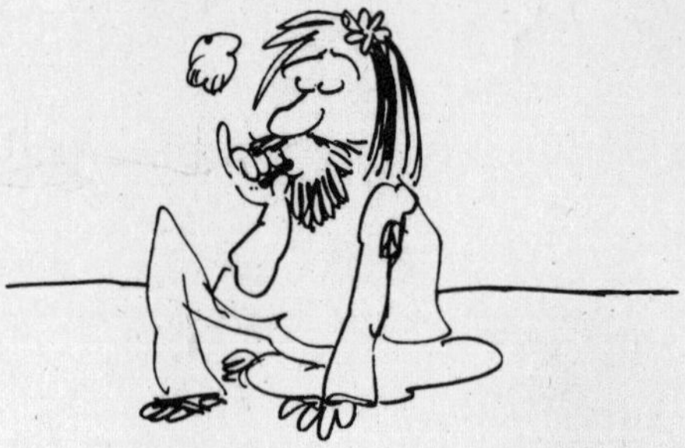

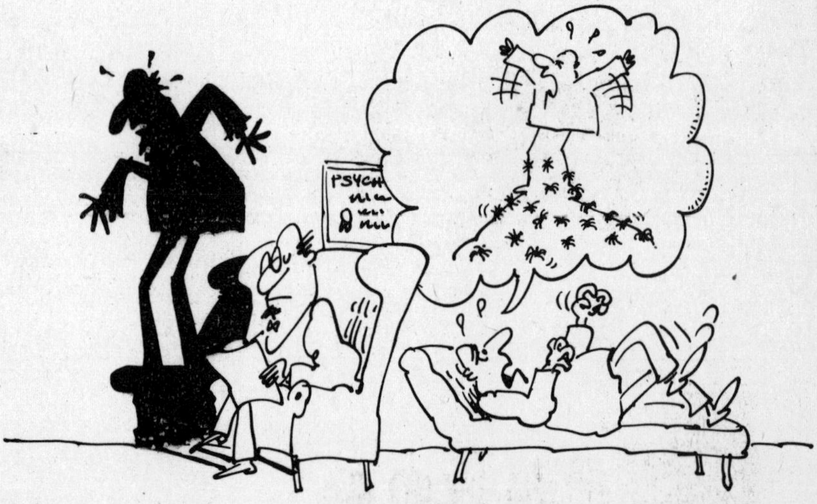

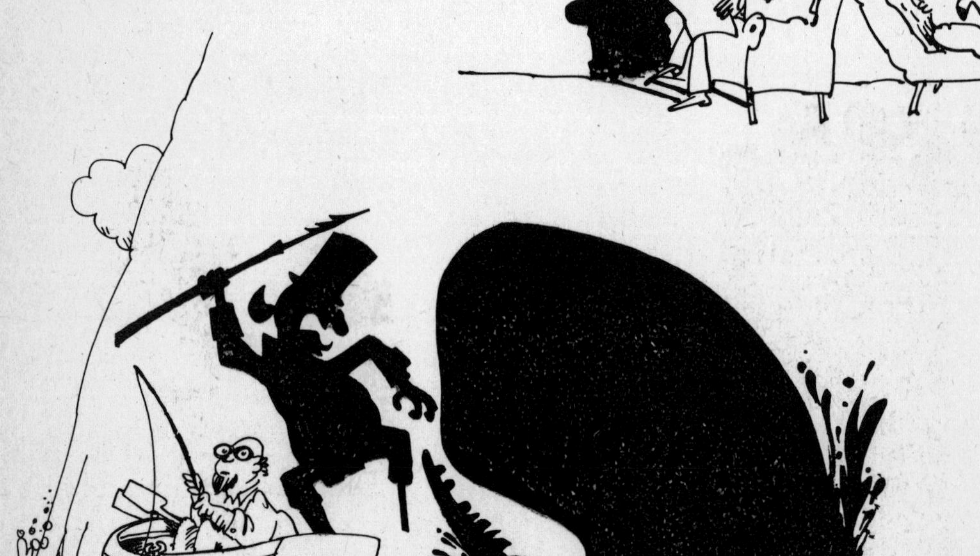